This book
belongs to

THIS IS SADIE

Sara O'Leary

with illustrations by **Julie Morstad**

Tundra Books

This is Sadie.

No, not that. That's a box.
Sadie is inside the box.

Wait, do you hear?
Sadie says she's not inside the box at all.
"I'm on an enormous boat," she says,
"crossing a wide, wide sea."

Here is Sadie now.

She's looking for land.

Only she's not looking too hard.

Sadie sails all the way round her room,
and back again.
And it still isn't even time for breakfast.

Sadie has learned to be quiet in the mornings
because old people need a lot of sleep.

When it is time to start the day,
Sadie tidies her room.

And then she chooses a dress.

"Don't tell the others," she whispers,
"but you are my favorite."

Sadie's perfect day is spent with friends.
Some of them live on her street,
and some live in the pages of books.

Sadie has been a girl who lived under the sea.

She has been a boy raised by wolves.

Sadie has had adventures in Wonderland.

And she has played the hero
in the world of fairy tales.

This is Sadie.

You probably think it's a tree, don't you?

It is, but way, way up at the top is Sadie,

chit-chatting with the birds.

Sadie has wings, of course.

They are just very, very hard to see.

Still, she knows they are there.

Maybe you have them too.

Have you checked?

Sadie's wings can take her anywhere she wants to go.

And they always bring her home again.

The days are never long enough for Sadie.

So many things

to make

and do

and be.

Sadie likes to make boats of boxes
and castles out of cushions.
But more than anything she likes stories,
because you can make them from nothing at all.

This is Sadie.

And this is her story.

For my darling mother — s.o'l.

For Ida, the Sadie-est girl I know — j.m.

Text copyright © 2015 by Sara O'Leary
Illustrations copyright © 2015 by Julie Morstad

Published in Canada by Tundra Books, a division of Random House of Canada Limited,
One Toronto Street, Suite 300, Toronto, Ontario m5c 2v6

Published in the United States by Tundra Books of Northern New York,
P.O. Box 1030, Plattsburgh, New York 12901

Library of Congress Control Number: 2014941840

Library and Archives Canada Cataloguing in Publication
O'Leary, Sara, author
This is Sadie / Sara O'Leary ; illustrated by Julie Morstad.
Issued in print and electronic formats.
ISBN 978-1-77049-532-6 (bound).—ISBN 978-1-77049-533-3 (epub)
I. Morstad, Julie, illustrator II. Title.
PS8579.L293T45 2015   JC813'.54   C2014-903067-3   C2014-903068-1

Edited by Tara Walker
Designed by Kelly Hill

The artwork in this book was rendered in gouache, watercolor and pencil crayon.
The text was set in Van Dijck.

www.tundrabooks.com

Printed and bound in China

2   3   4   5   6   19   18   17   16   15

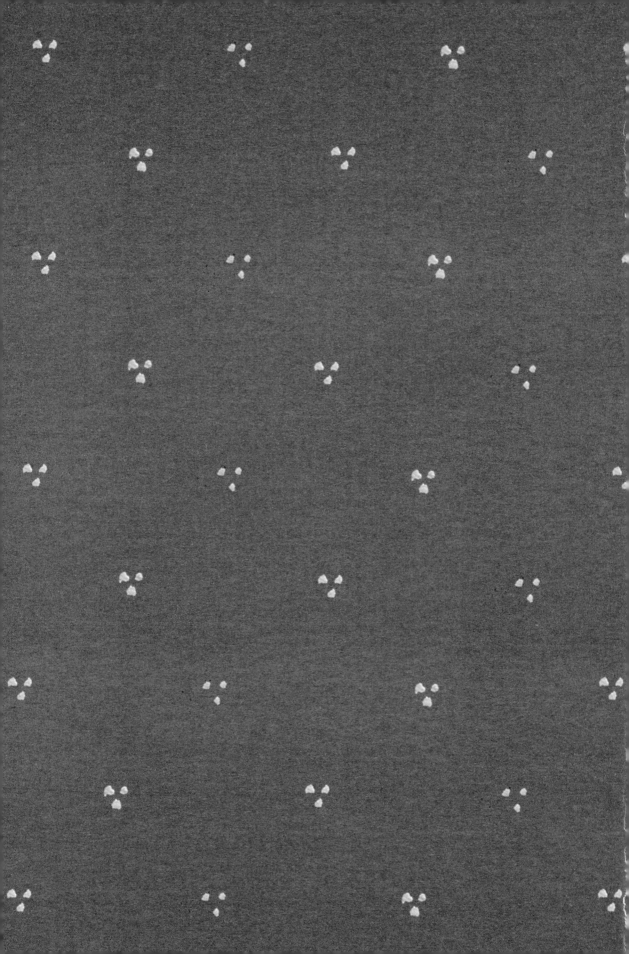